THEY MARCHED UNDER THE SUN

CRIS JUDAR

TRANSLATED BY
LARA NORGAARD

Fonograf Editions
Edited by Adie B. Steckel, Jeff Alessandrelli, Ellena Basada
Portland, OR & New York City, NY

Cover art by Dennis Foster
Cover and text design by Mike Corrao

First Edition, First Printing
FONO45

Published by Fonograf Editions
www.fonografeditions.com

For information about permission to reuse any material from this
book, please contact Fonograf Ed. at info@fonografeditions.com.

Distributed by NYU Press
NYUPress.org

The manufacturer's authorized representative in the EU for product
safety is Mare Nostrum Group B.V., Mauritskade 21D, 1091 GC
Amsterdam, The Netherlands.
Email: gpsr@mare-nostrum.co.uk.

[clmp]

Fonograf Editions is a proud member of the Community
of Literary Magazines and Presses

ISBN: 978-1-964499-63-5
ISBN (ebook): 978-1-964499-64-2
LCCN: 2025949931

THEY MARCHED UNDER THE SUN

FONO GRAF

FONOGRAF EDITIONS

Every woman
A POLITICAL PRISONER
Every woman
A POLITICAL PRISONER
You are political prisoner
LOCKED IN TENSE BODY
You are political prisoner
LOCKED IN STIFF MIND
You are political prisoner
LOCKED TO YOUR PARENTS
You are political prisoner
LOCKED TO YOUR PAST
Free yourself
FREE YOURSELF

DIANE DI PRIMA
Revolutionary Letter #49

In the search for a place in the sun
When there's nearly no sunlight
Blood rushes to the landscape
And invades fields, cities, and relationships
with the worst kind of red
There's a big war in the world
There are little wars
Myths, microtones, intermediaries, hybrids
that give balance to the arid earth
with words staked in dirt
made into flags
used to create borders
These are the front lines of our days

INTRODUCTION

"When we read a text, we are either read by the text or we are in the text. Either we tame the text, we ride on it, or we are swallowed up by it, as by a whale."
—Helène Cixous, *Reading with Clarice Lispector*

For novelist Cris Judar, language and bodies are charged with conventions and social norms, and as such, language and bodies contain within them the potential for social upheaval and change. They are sites of repression, erasure, and enclosure, but also spaces for liberation, creativity, and dissident expression. Language constructs and reinforces our political infrastructures, but fiction has the capacity to estrange us from language, to imagine new experiences of embodiment, expand horizons of expectation, and open possibilities for ways of being, of moving through the world. Fiction also has the ability to show how language snaps under the weight of violence, how trauma ruptures the very meaning of words.

These intertwined thematic threads—language and the body, social and political repression, and lines of flight towards liberation—coalesce in Cris Judar's fiction. A non-binary author from São Paulo, they are part of a generation of writers on the front lines of critiquing and challenging the politics of gender and sexuality in contemporary Brazil, where much as in the United States today, trans rights, queer identities, feminism, as well as the language we use to speak about gender stand at the forefront of political struggle. Judar, who has published nearly half a dozen works of fiction including award-winning books *Roteiros para uma vida curta* and *Oito do Sete*, approaches these political topics through genre-defying prose that hovers about the borders of poetry, playing at the limits of the vocabularies and grammars used to define bodies, desire, and femininity.

The queer poetics Judar advances are rooted in Brazilian politics, past and present. That specificity is especially evident in *They Marched Under the Sun*, where abuses of the Brazilian state fold into intimate narratives. The book is structured around the voices of two young women in São Paulo, Ana and Joan, each on the cusp of their eighteenth birthday, each experimenting with their sense of self, with their limits and possibilities. But their voices are not alone. To the contrary, their interlocked narrative arcs are constantly interrupted by traces of far broader social trauma. In letters that appear throughout the novel, women imprisoned under the Brazilian military dictatorship (1964-1985) who experienced gendered violence and extrajudicial imprisonment at the hands of the state also grasp at new vocabularies, reimagining what it means to inhabit their bodies, to experience desire in the wake of torture. In the case of a letter from the character Julia F. Dantos, these new vocabularies are literal: "Legs = flamingos. Buttocks = fluffy clouds. Eyes = egg yolks, unbeaten. Lips = highways, leading me towards desirable destinations. Neck = a sunset overlook. My body = a satellite, poised for discovery."

By including these voices, Judar explores the intimate corners of Brazilian history, and they also point to the gendered dimensions of state violence. Brazil's rightwing, Cold War dictatorship hunted down citizens perceived as communists or leftists, deeming them enemies of the state, but like many other authoritarian regimes, it also upheld strict norms around gender and traditional family values. LGBTQ communities were persecuted, feminism repressed, and discourses around sexuality that did not conform to conservative Christian ideals censored. The violence and torture that took place in detention centers were also gendered, as women suffered abuses different from those to which men were subjected. Through intimate reflections on the body, Judar's novel unpacks how dictatorships are forces that impose straightjacketed ideas of morality, and how present-day social norms carry the weight of our past political systems, as well as the legacies of those who managed to live in its crevices, asserting a nonconformist existence.

Indeed, the social traumas of *They Marched Under the Sun* are not only echoes of a past regime. The novel also alludes to contemporary examples of violence in the country's current, democratic system, gesturing to the ways in which brutality persists in Brazil as state and corporate power continue to commit violence with near impunity. In "October" (the novel's chapters are labeled by month, not by number), Ana looks into her reflection in a mirror and is confronted by a voice cataloguing the deluge of violence in Brazil from the past decade: "river dams ruptured" refers to the Brumadinho dam disaster in Minas Gerais, when technical failures at a nearby mining facility caused a massive mudslide, burying hundreds of mine workers, animals, and residents of the nearby town alive. "One hundred and eleven rounds fired; five boys dead" alludes to the police killing of five teenagers in a poor neighborhood of Rio de Janeiro in which officers fired 111 bullets at their targets in a gross excess of brute force. "Dandara, the *travesti*" references a case of the violent hate crimes that *travestis* in Brazil suffer on a regular basis. The term *travesti*—which I left untranslated given its specificity to Latin America—describes a person who was assigned male at birth, holds a female gender identity, and lives in a context of social and economic precarity and exclusion due to that identity, which has sex work on the streets as its main reference (currently, the term has acquired strong political associations and has also been adopted by trans people in different contexts). Dandara dos Santos was tortured and beaten to death by a group of twelve people, who eventually tossed her body in a wheelbarrow, shot her, and posted a video of the crime on social media. "The thirteen bullets that took Marielle" speaks to the 2018 political assassination of Marielle Franco, a Black, socialist, lesbian city councilperson in Rio de Janeio and vocal critic of police brutality who was killed after giving a speech, leading to nationwide outrage and protests. "A routine police search over Luana Barbosa's butch body" describes the killing of a Black, gay woman, a mother from the periphery of São Paulo, who died at the hands of the police as a result of blunt force trauma, after asserting her right to have a body search carried out by a female police officer.

None of the examples in this catalogue are easily translated or transposed into another language and social context; they are utterly specific to Brazil, and Judar's choice to include them is an act of denunciation grounded in a particular history and political context, one that engulfs their characters. At the same time, there are clear resonances between this novel's political outcry and demands to recognize repression against queer and trans communities, against workers, people of color, and other marginalized groups far beyond Brazil. Indeed, despite its specificity, *They Marched Under the Sun* has had an unusually global trajectory since its original publication in Brazil in

2021. Unlike most authors, for whom translation into English is a steppingstone towards publication in other languages, especially those in the Global South, *They Marched Under the Sun* was translated into Egyptian Arabic and Italian—and other stories in Judar's oeuvre into Indonesian, Italian, German, Danish, and Spanish—prior to my embarking on this English translation. Judar's prose may be resistant to translation in the way it reasserts its contextual rootedness, but the political issues and themes of the novel are nevertheless broadly relevant, compelling to audiences across wide swaths of the world. And the urgency of Judar's meditations on authoritarianism, impunity, social repression, and avenues for liberation in the United States in 2026 is so clear as to be self-evident.

But another, equally significant reason as to why we should read Judar in English translation lies in language. In 1990, French feminist theorist Helène Cixous wrote a series of essays on Brazilian author Clarice Lispector in which she articulated the importance of reading novels originally written in foreign languages. If part of feminism involves transgression within language—or what Cixous describes as an effort at becoming "transgrammatical"—then looking at what kinds of experimentation take place in other countries and languages is indispensable to breaking bounds in any mother tongue. She writes, from the French context, "it is good to work on foreign texts—Clarice Lispector's, James Joyce's and others'—because they displace our relation to grammar. In everything we do, we are questioning femininity. We work on texts as quests, that is, a questioning of femininity, on traces that are perceptible." Traces of femininity appear throughout *They Marched Under the Sun*, sometimes in ways that are best left untranslated—such as in the case of *travesti*—and in others, that weave their way through novel images redefining desire in English: "To love is to fill one lung with suffering and the other with stones. A belly full of otters, a leg of lamas, rump like a basket of gold that could fit a calf or whole human child."

It is apt to engage *They Marched Under the Sun* as though it were a quest, because the idea of questioning femininity, of questioning the ties between language and bodies, is central to Judar's agenda. This is the very quest that Ana and Joan themselves embark on at the outset of the narrative. It is the quest that is meditated on in fables and fantastical stories that appear throughout the book, such as the anecdote about a community of people determined to transform themselves into cats: "they lifted their tailbones towards the moon while lapping cream from fine chinaware; they meowed in a chorus of tones and practiced their purrs, which weren't all that convincing; they frequented polemical lectures on the subject of The Art of Becoming a Feline-Human-Citizen, or How to Live Well as a Soul Separated from the Body." Ana, Joan, and even the community of cat people fostering this feline culture—all of these fictional characters seek to embrace an estranged relationship to their bodies, to the Portuguese language, to socially imposed conventions of being. Reading with Judar in English is an opportunity to question and transgress, to imagine worlds and words of possibility closer to home.

LARA NORGAARD

JANUARY

Ana, twelve months before her eighteenth birthday

Passed hand to hand in biology class, the dried beetle exoskele-ton defied the claim that only men are capable of achieving certain heights in the area of design. I wasn't sure what that thing was made of, but it was hard to believe its solid, mathematical structure was caused by nature and not expert calculations.

Unlike Clark, the beetle didn't make me feel revulsion or pity. This surprised me.

About Clark: a person in miniature, preserved in a glass jar filled with formaldehyde, displayed alongside other vials on the shelf of the high school science lab.

About anatomy and destiny: Clark is a protagonist, the focal point for students who felt guilty about his inexistence, which was subaqueous for the benefit of our education.

About me: in one of the most widely known versions of myself, I seemed disinterested in Clark. In secret, however, I'd long observed the pink former-futureman with his puny curled-up legs. When the room was empty, flooded with that light typical of liminal spaces, I imagined virtuous futures for the tiny mass of cartilage: a frustrated attempt to become someone, to wear jeans, to make social media profiles, to go out for drinks, had he survived. Infinite possibilities lost in the haze of the current moment. And the reason why he was terminated will never be known.

About the dead beetle, dry and stiff: it was as though nature had created its own version of the material we know as plastic. That's why the insect was so soothing, in the same way a piece of plastic can be.

The whole thing began in my yard that same morning. The rain stopped, infinite drops of water reflected blades of grass, and I spotted an unusual stone in the plot of begonias. Were the scene to be filmed from above, the begonias would look like a stack of red apples. With a closer look, I was able to identify the stone as the body-coffin of an enormous insect, on its back, in a state of surrender, radiant, inky obsidian. I snatched the jewel, took it for myself.

Pause the scene for a moment. Suspending reality for a quick but detailed analysis, it becomes clear that the three of us were connected somehow, more or less like this: (1) the image of a dead beetle, reduced to its irresistibly aesthetic exoskeleton; (2) the figure of Clark, who wouldn't have the opportunity to seize life beyond his fate, which was similar to that of the insect: "dying to become an object of analysis for middle class youth"; (3) me, a 17-year-old girl who didn't know if she wanted to be more like the beetle [memory and form] or Clark [aberration and impossibility]. And with that, the dilemma had been set before me.

Clark

She's crazy about black hairclips, crazy enough that she collects them. Even with my vision blurred by glass and liquid, I can see them carefully arranged in her hair like large, lacquered bugs. I'd even venture to say that she comes over to me so that I can admire those clips more than for any other reason. They're always shiny, in different shapes and sizes. Purely a fetish object, which is something she knows nothing about. I know a lot of things, even though I'm an embryo. Mystics would claim that my memories come from past lives, but I'd say it's just *cellular memory*. I carry stories in my physical composition – luckily for me, all properly preserved in formaldehyde. I'm more alive and alert than most people walking around out there. Like that girl, the hairclip exhibitionist, for example. I feel sorry for her. Human loneliness moves me. My former-futuremom is Estela Ramos, and she was that girl's age when she conceived me. Mom taught me lots of things, but she had to give me up in order to stay in school. They said it was a reasonable trade: a huge quantity of shame, an amount that no single body could hold, in exchange for the virtue of donating a tiny quantity of flesh, a body-child, for the benefit of the students who would define the future. And so here I am, a little pearl reaching its boiling point. A pink bud with potential for nuclear bloom. I know that I will leave this place the day that all those imprisoned on

Earth are released and those who are free are taken prisoner. I carry that revelation for those who are curious to know. I am the seed that will sprout. Indeed, I've already screamed this truth at the girl with insects in her hair, who seemed to listen attentively, brazenly. She nicknamed me Clark and wrote the name on the label of my flask. I can read it backwards from inside my aquatic cell: KRALC. To be honest, I'd have preferred to be named after a Pharaoh or an Egyptian god; it would be a better match for what I am, for what I will become.

Joan, twelve months before her eighteenth birthday

I smoked and embalmed bodies with my grandmother. I know that bodies become gems when left underground. People at burials always think the opposite—that shame is cast over human remains if a final resting place isn't dignified. But I maintain: bodies give the ground value. Like a sapphire sunk into mud, a buried corpse hidden from view brings the surrounding dirt a kind of meaning, a warm, pulsating, valuable core.

In the norms around bodily death, in the pedagogy that permeates dying, there exists a trajectory, an initiation marked by beginnings. One learns the arithmetic of color, the active properties of beeswax, of camphor and cedar oil, of palm wine, all natural shrouds for a death that tries to remain alive, as in the time of the pharaohs.

I was prepared to work with the unexpected, with smells that disconcert and textures that usually trigger hysteria or the urge to flee. I'd been trained in these matters since I was seven years old. My grandmother passed sprigs of herbs, putrefying animals, fistfuls of moist earth, algae soaked in still water, rotted eggs and fruits, and fish innards beneath my nostrils and blindfolded eyes.

Exposed as I was to the inconvenience of these socially unacceptable smells, I was eventually able to cope with the surprises of our finite bodies, their ligatures, their fluids and insides, always varied in form and content. Only trained hands can touch the uninterrupted transformation of decomposition. During those years, I formed the knots and sketched out the traces that make up who I am today. I learned what it means to be alive: in essence, an accumulation of successive deaths.

I wish I could choose existence without torture. To opt for my bones and flesh—even the material from which my spirit is composed— to fuse into a more admissible version of myself: acceptable, part of the system. I live in Brazil, in some swath of time between the 1960s and 70s. My imagination remains there, in that moment. My thoughts don't inhabit a house or a cell; like days, years, or decades, they can at most stay temporarily sheltered. Fluid things can't be held prisoner. As for my body, such an easy thing to capture, they've done nearly everything to it. Tossed it around, mistreated it, dunked it in tanks of water. I replied to their countless questions, repeated answers ad infinitum with only slight variations in phrasing and word choice: it was a game of cyphers and codes developed simply to confuse me.

They demanded surprising precision from someone turned inside out. As though someone reduced to scraps and fragments would be capable of emitting coherent and articulate speech. First came the man with a harsh voice. Then came the other one; he cast a blinding light into my eyes, which I had to keep open. I resisted as they pushed, giving them nothing. Days passed, and while they washed me in a barrel of water so murky that my menstrual blood couldn't be seen, an enemy paid me a visit. He spoke kind words, told me that he wanted to be close to me, fall in love with me, and asked me to stay by his side. That's when I heard screams nearby, a bit of commotion. New flesh had arrived in the basement.

I thought about dawn, about salty waves, about spotted jaguars tearing through a jungle. I ran while I was tied to a chair, hooked up to electric currents, unmoored with no land in sight.

Orders came from higher-up, and I was transferred to a real prison. Their reasons remain a mystery to me. I stayed there for three years and reunited with the future father of my son, who was conceived between walls and metal bars. I had a vision that water enveloped his tiny body. Not my waters, but a chemical, artificial liquid. If he'd been born on solid earth, he would have become a leader, I'm certain of that.

I started over when I reached the first year of the second half of my existence. I always try to create new beginnings, but my thoughts were laden with the evils I acquired during that swatch of time stuck in the 1960s and 70s. Now we're in the 21st century and it's hard to manage all the numbers my body has hosted. Let's be real: numbers and calculations were never my strong suit.

Estela Ramos

FEBRUARY

OPENING SHOT.
The screen fades to reveal the Molishop product logo, prominently centered.

CUT TO: A wide angle shot of a busy street. A tall blonde woman in a white tube top and high heels strolls down the sidewalk. Heads turn; men look over their shoulders to watch her walk by.

CUT TO: A close-up of the Body Sculpture Electric Waistband secured around the blonde's hips. Radiant, she lowers her blouse. The belt is completely hidden.

The blonde cheerily goes for a drive, tosses a few blocks of wood into her living room fireplace, chats on the phone, gets a manicure, works on her laptop, pets her yellow lab.

CUT TO: A shot of the electric waistband, overlayed with graphics. Red arrows run from right to left, then left to right, emphasizing the effectiveness of Molishop's technology.

The blonde answers her phone. She swishes over to the door and takes a package from a delivery man, who's also smiling.

CUT TO: A black screen. The "Molishop" logo and phone number appear momentarily, flashing in a bold, vibrant red font.

VOICEOVER (OFF CAMERA):

Looking for the perfect body? You better be ready to sweat through your shirt! But wait: what if you could make getting in shape something fun and sexy? Now you can with the new Body Sculpture Electric Waistband from Molishop. Using micro-rhythmic vibrations, this belt shapes your hips and tightens your waist, leaving you with the figure you always dreamed of. With a few minutes of training each day, you'll find your body transformed into a slender, healthy hourglass shape and catch admirers left and right! Make those pesky rolls of fat disappear and watch your true silhouette come to life. No need to step foot in the gym!

The Body Sculpture Electric Waistband from Molishop uses exclusive Fitmaster technology, which calculates the optimal level of compression to burn off surplus body fat. The perfect body, guaranteed!

Call now to get your Body Sculpture Electric Waistband TODAY and receive a one-time only, early release deal. Buy one Body Sculpture Electric Waistband, get one free! It's the perfect gift for your mother, sister, or friend! What are you waiting for? Call before stock runs out!

Ana

The telemarketing channel bellowed at me, trying to make me feel like I needed one of the shuddering little belts that promises a suggestive silhouette with mere minutes of effort each day. The idea didn't so much as tickle my curiosity. I felt no need to exaggerate my curves and fill out my favorite outfit, which I wore every afternoon: worn-out shorts, a t-shirt, and socks in clashing colors, studded with Cheeto crumbs. That sprinkle of vertiginous orange also added a touch of color to the living room couch. The satin upholstery patterned with white flowers was once my mom's prized possession. Then a year went by, and suddenly all she could think about was switching it out for a terracotta-toned chenille. Mothers tend to become obsessed with specific objects. Once they obtain those objects, an accelerated process of emotional detachment takes place, which contributes to the thing in question falling rapidly into disrepair. It's not so unlike how human relationships unravel. In that context, the scattered remains of my favorite snack were convenient, and I, in some small way, had done my part.

A tube of mascara, some blush, a 4D eyeshadow kit, and half-used lipstick: that was all my mom had passed down to me. *You need a bit of color,* she declared to my pasty face. I didn't see the point in painting my skin or compressing my frame into sinuous shapes; what I wanted was a body open to the world, one with no clear beginning or ending. That's what I told Oswald, looking back at him through our reflection in the mirror. My brother lived as himself, without artifice, and like him I felt no desire to succumb to ornaments, cover-ups, and disguises, the reduction of certain parts of my body and augmentation of others. Disjointed and limitless, full of edges and dotted lines, I chose to reject all such interventions.

I ended up using the eyeshadow kit on paper, like watercolors. I produced good work in that period. The fluidity of colors in movement was what I needed, and I painted for the gaze of anyone who might absorb the figures I created, sowing seeds for reflection.

It felt as though women—at least, all the women around me—were aesthetically destined for caricature. I wanted them to leave me alone with my hair clips, my perennial obsession. By parting my hair into four or five sections, separating each with uniquely positioned clips, I didn't run the risk of suffering stagnant or repetitive thoughts. That was my juvenile logic, the millennial law I decreed. Let humanity leave me be with my enormous imagination. I was born with a spirit that runs in reverse, and I'd do just about anything to stay that way.

Joan

The dead can be people, and the dead can be ideas and revolutions buried in a hurry, before they have the chance to bloom and definitively change the order of things. The dead can be women, buried alive because of the simple fact that no one sees them. In reality, they are planets and deities, the depths of the ocean, everything that is uncountable and impossible to measure.

A legend I carry with me: long ago, in the distant past, there was an old woman who lived in the desert and sucked on the bones she came across in her wanderings. Lit candles adorned the insides of her aging body. As the heat of her guts poured over bone marrow, the old woman filled her belly with flesh and stories, in a process utterly different from the way mankind eats to survive. Deserts are oceans that went extinct; skeletons turned into shells and, much later, became bodies. A small miracle.

She was amazed by how many bones the land had accumulated. One could guess the bones had belonged to women because of the shapes they left imprinted in the sand. The old crone was a gardener of calcified flowers, moving gingerly as though to avoid stepping on eggshells. That waterless plot held a rare, diversified archive. Drought can sprout life and store temporalities, though we've been made to think otherwise. Day after day, she watered inert jewels with air and fire, walking with a rhythmic gate and humming in a voice so hoarse it seemed to pour from the origins of the earth. From that place: all events are ideas that escaped from linear projections of reality, like pollen suspended in the air, in a ray of sunlight that never lands in one place. She observed the bones as though she were caressing them. She exhaled ash and brought back into being what had been lost—not just bodies but also their oceanic beauty, things held in movement, defining existence not through limits but in the geometry of waves, in the scent of salt.

MARCH

Ana

The sky was a sticky, liquid blur, offering hardly any comfort on a day beaten down by road signs rushing by in a rapid sequence. The numbers were so out of focus that I couldn't tell if we were getting close to the beach. The car stopped. The slowly setting sun acted as a traffic signal, letting us know how important it was to continue down the curved highway, which looked as though it had been clipped from a sportscar ad. Oswald and I sat in the back; up front, mom was with dad, confident he'd given his family everything they desired. Summer has a way of inspiring parents and poets.

After a few more miles, we finally parked. We set down suitcases and let our arms fall by our sides, opened the windows of the house at random, and boiled water for dinner. Sprawled across the leopard print rug, I scrolled through messages on my phone. Flecks of synthetic fabric got caught in my belly button.

I was much more than the sum of data points on my profile. There, two breasts nested against a butt, which stood beside an image of lips, an image of thighs. All appropriately enlarged, with the aim of attracting attention on that cheap podium offered to people my age. Because older women are invisible—at least the withered ones, if not those who preserve certain parts of their body in rigid, exaggerated proportions. Theirs is a feat comparable to building ambitious skyscrapers in Dubai, where architectural miracles tower over water as temperatures soar above 50 degrees Celsius. These projects demand extensive financial investment, an army of day laborers, and an indefinite time horizon—resources that people with finite existences, bodies, and pockets find nearly impossible to obtain.

I knew that the way others placed value on me was correlated to the ratio of soft and hard parts of my body. Flesh idealized as soft should not be hard, and vice-versa. In a modern-day witch hunt, any inversion of the rule is ruled inadequate. Anything that pours or drips from our bodies is judged within the same rigid, intolerant standards. This was the moment in my life when I became conscious of my own fluids, of the red that remained inside my internal circuits, the red that broke loose from me.

When we got to the beach, I became part of the ocean we were visiting. I had summer in my gait, in the awkward provisional pad I'd bought in a hurry at a highway rest stop. Mass production never fit me very well. Cotton and the color white can't contain fluid waters or curb my nature: expansive, full of movement.

It was a formative time for me, that vacation. I understood all at once how disconnected my appearance was from the expectations that surrounded me. I was composed of dynamic images, like the wings of the dragonfly I captured in a glass on the veranda one evening that summer. Her survival instinct was quick and urgent. I observed her from the other side of the glass, just as I'd done with Clark.

Her pain was my desire. Her existence in the void mirrored the suspension of my own reality. I wanted to take all of that beauty, the accelerated, pendular movements against the walls of a transparent cell, the eternity that comes before a final breath, and hold it in the empty air. I wanted to carve the beauty and desperation of a swan song sped up in pursuit of death into my retinas.

So delicate, her voiceless scream. The last seconds of that symphony of tiny wings came together in irresistible agony. With all reserves of resistance spent, she fell still. I went to bed with a weight on my chest, even though I was thankful to have witnessed her final, magnificent performance.

Joan

There was a lady who lived in the trunk of a windswept tree. She was a mixture of milk and sap, but she revealed herself to me in her solid state, wearing a wide-brimmed green hat and holding a banana leaf fan, her curly brown hair in ringlets. Her amber blouse was tucked into a tight black A-line skirt. In her hand she held a chalice, and whisps of smoke poured from its rim.

A parrot lived on her right shoulder; a monocle was perched before her left eye. I saw her every time I drank a potion, her appearance differing only slightly from one meeting to the next. She never said a word, but I could hear her speak. Who knows how I heard what she said or why I was sure that she was the one who arranged every path forward, but I knew each vision appeared only with her permission.

Grandma had given me my first potion.

She told me to pinch my nose because of the taste, but I found it hard to down the cup without breathing. I drank the full dose of bitter, swampy, viscous, and hardly-liquid dirt. It coursed through my body, cleansing my hollow, intimate spaces.

Submerged in a plasma of vegetal cells and surrounded by the earthy scent of damp leaves, I latched onto the conscience of buried treasures and connected with the upward thrust of a plant in growth, my floodgates bursting open. A tambourine sounded in the distance.

I glimpsed entire cities pulsing with movement, their transportation networks moving an unthinkable number of people. So many heads accumulated, one next to the other, as green and gold lights gleamed from locomotive creatures borne from iron, steam, and noise, their throats rumbling as humans sprinted to catch up in a tempo set by their bosses, all so these people wouldn't have time to think of their basic needs. On a tower, a clock of enormous dimensions waved its unruly hands. The clock was king.

I then observed innumerable women holding tambourines and trumpets, adorned with handkerchiefs and ceremonial paint, releasing melodious cries and holding up vellum inscribed with characters I wouldn't read; they carried children, they fought for one another, for many, for all, loving each other. They wore dresses and trousers and occupied the same urban arteries dominated by those ironclad, wheeled animals. They marched under the sun. In this procession, for those who kissed as in a clap of thunder, as in a revolt, in the light step of those who manage to keep walking while caught in an embrace, and who, even with their eyes closed, have the sharpest sense of direction.

For them, shouts went unheard (*you will die, now, forever*) because they sustained fire on their lips and their lips on their words, their words in conviction and conviction in every step, a tremor in each gesture, composing a cosmic symphony on the concrete that carried words of liberation to all people. The hate sourced from dry rivers was flattened under the feverish feet of all of those people.

The rhythmic beat stopped.

I was sitting on the ground when I regained consciousness. It felt good to sense blood sliding through my veins in parallel to seeds sprouting in the soil beneath me. I learned that I would feed the planet with infusions of my body and spirit. It was at that moment that I started to produce, not just consume.

ON BLOOD AND ABSORPTION
A study by Lena Rivas

Observation (1): a type of bleach-white magic capable of containing menstrual blood was crafted by the hands of men. First invented to restrain the body's outpourings, the device is made up of cotton and synthetic fibers, dissolved in copper and aluminum tanks at 8,568 feet above sea level. After a lengthy fermentation and dissolution process (this takes nearly eight months), a residual paste is transferred into concave moonstone encasements, where it is held while all remaining liquid has dripped through a massive stainless-steel sieve. The leftover stuff is used to construct floodgates at the thresholds of those who menstruate.

Observation (2): one must amplify and synthesize the song of 399 white-feathered birds in order to manufacture the same number of absorbent insertions for industrial & commercial production. A user of these materials is at risk of losing a limb, should they suffer from the rare but nevertheless possible *shock produced by elements with highly conflicting compositions*, a condition caused by using hygiene products designed to purify human bodies. These are the lengths people go to in order to hide blood, so that men won't feel nausea, rage, or disgust.

Observation (3): 578 glacial peaks melt, compromising the energetic clarity of the atmosphere and stunning aerial landscapes featured in advertisements (top-notch selling points for a rapidly warming global tourism industry). This produces the energy needed to manufacture devices and appendages aimed at effectively eliminating menstrual cycles. Since anything that changes dramatically results in discomfort. Since respectability means staying in a straight line, without peaks or valleys, waves or detours. One company replaces the next in a continuous effort to achieve the ideal of predictability: static, desirable bodies devoid of fluids.

Observation (4): in 957 jars made of pure crystal, one must store the cries of more than twenty bird species hunted in remote regions in order to produce pills capable of withholding the scream, the grind, the tears, and the fury of those in their days of bleeding. After the first phase (open-jar-pack-bird-songs-close-lid), the compressed song becomes a knoll of powder, an amalgam of powerful chemicals (like chlorine, which turns the substance a bright white). In the final stage, the powder is poured into capsules and then ingested once every morning and once every night, or as needed. Companies guarantee that the mouths of people who consume the appropriate dosage will emit only niceties and strangled opinions—aside from the occasional sharp, low-pitched little croon.

I was a political prisoner in 1968, and I was tortured. But that doesn't mean I permanently lost my libido. I simply needed to re-name my body parts in order to build associations with nice things, with pleasant images.

Legs = flamingos. Buttocks = fluffy clouds. Eyes = egg yolks, unbeaten. Lips = highways, leading me towards desirable destinations. Neck = a sunset overlook. My body = a satellite, poised for discovery.

When it comes to desire, I realized that it's a feeling that walks along sections of my body overlooked by scientific, industrial, corporate, and religious interpretations of pleasure.

Through exercises in which fiction comes into contact with reality, I came to write my own script for lust and satisfaction, ignoring what people say is correct or ideal.

It's undeniable: a writer who is tortured has a different experience than a tortured cook or a tortured engineer. But those alternatives push me to imagine interesting possibilities for new beginnings, assuming the cook and the engineer should wish for them, drawing on the full force of their abilities.

Some say I'm very rational, and that's why I was able to overcome everything I endured with some of my sanity intact. Maybe my new vocabulary is my way of acting crazy, the only weapon left in my arsenal. It's not easy to find someone capable of cracking the code to my fragmented, convoluted glossary. It's as though my body has become an indecipherable, unintelligible sarcophagus.

Julia F. Dantos

APRIL

Ana

The cassette gazed at me with vintage eyes. Tiny flashback eyes made from two reels, which people like my dad would twist and twist with a pencil whenever the tape was stuck. A few minutes of happiness depended on a pen lodged in an orifice lined with little teeth. When it worked (which it generally did), the tape replayed the song that everyone loved; the body of the cassette was home to music, venerated like a pagan god to whom we offered glue, saliva, and adhesive tape in exchange for immediate regeneration. If it weren't for that tape, my deepest truths would have never awakened within me, stimulated by sounds from other eras, trapped in an object unfamiliar to my generation.

I knew full well that the boy wanted to eat my heart. We weren't cold and we weren't vampires, but we were dazed by a system that swallowed us whole. In other words, we were seventeen. We talked and listened to music for hours. Primp's most attractive quality was his mouth, with his teeth encased in tiny stainless-steel cages. I imagined that fugitive words might reveal whatever hid behind those metallic cells at precisely the right moment.

Straight teeth are important for a nice, respectable appearance, my mom said.

Better teeth, better speech, my dad added.

Perfect teeth: radiant smiles, a dive into a bright blue swimming pool, and the seduction of many lovers, advertisers told me.

A line of evenly shaped pearly teeth leads to a good job, a secure path in life, society confirmed.

Metal started encasing the conversations I had with Primp, probably because I desired him. I could make out complex structures spanning the room whenever we spent time together: fine as the thinnest wire, they floated before our eyes, malleable and airy, forming intricate webs and infinite geometric patterns. Anything of value that we uttered went inside these structures, stored as in a birdcage or a cloud, vessels more trustworthy than flimsy human memories. Our ideas had a definitive register that I could access whenever I wanted.

Some prisons are liberating for things that can flourish and grow in captivity. It requires a heightened sensitivity to comprehend the intensity of existence in extreme confinement, to recognize that the imprisoned person is offered an impossibility of boundaries. Not many people think about it, but I've been preoccupied by thoughts like this for some time now, developing theories on the subject. From prison to prison, new kinds of freedom form, for those on the outside and for those within. New horizons emerge from restriction.

I made an Instagram profile, and it was like a hyper-exposed cell flipped on its head. I could reveal only what I wanted to and generate controversial opinions and selfies from all sorts of angles, all while hiding the true, fragile parts of me. At times, I felt like a jar of jam on sale in the supermarket. Unlike Clark, I only revealed the opposite of what I was, with pictures that drew the eye to my hairclips, which looked like prehistoric insects embalmed in glue, tar, and varnish. My mouth clasped shut, I baffled my viewers.

Coating my head in eye-catching adornments, no one could read my mind. This was my greatest triumph by far.

Joan

(On heat and fire)

For those who come home on a chilly night, watching firewood burn on a wood stove can be a moment of enlightenment, opening parts of the soul that shouldn't be hindered or neglected. Everything happens through an unfolding of images and sensations: stove, bread, a hot sun, shelter, a glimpse of the end of a tunnel, distance from death, a dilated pupil, the smell of smoke, of extracted essence, of charcoal.

During rituals, or even in everyday life, the way candle wax melts should always be taken into account—if it drips everywhere, if it forms waves and wrinkles, slopes and channels, tiny sculptures and stalactites; if it's impossible to recognize something like people or wild beasts in the residue; if the wax falls in a semi-solid wax downpour or if it evaporates. That isn't to mention the flame, which I've seen turn double when twin forces are invoked at once: entity and god, goddess and animal, sap and trunk—the combinations are infinite.

I've heard a flame snap and tremble like fire from a dragon's nostrils.

You need to pause and observe in order to manage so many possibilities and their respective outcomes, as though you were launching a boat into a river's rushing current. A candle and the flame that consumes it are oracles driven by the intentions of the person who incited those forces and elements. They are ways of communicating, of interpreting and perceiving without spoken language. A sigh, a thought, a feeling are key ingredients, transformed into a prayer intuited by the inside of the tongue and palms turned upwards.

When I put on my first long, flowing skirt I could mold candle wax just by spinning counterclockwise in front of the flame. I determined my destiny, susceptible as it was to many winds. I conquered a recognizable, venerable body all for myself, under the same law that allows the bedrocks of mountain peaks to take shape or a wave to leave its trace on kilometer after kilometer of wet sand, forever indifferent to humans and their demands for production.

That night, grandma and I danced to Uncle Oscar playing the fiddle, and the flames danced too, licking at our skirts without setting the fabric on fire. Things were aflame but only in other forms: in the heat generated by the quick steps of our feet, expanding to fill the centers that organize life.

The light cast shadowy figures on the walls, mutants spinning continuously, always in tune with our movements. That's how we concluded each meal marking the change in seasons: with a party, a celebration honoring our ancestors.

We set aside portions of food as an offering to whichever deity ruled that day. The lady in the tree was always who I chose to honor. We adopted the gods we worshiped, just as they decided if they wished to appear to us.

Uncle Oscar

Joan is the daughter of birds, which means one could define her as the winged tenor of words. She lives alongside one hundred and one anonymous letters, which she herself transcribed: they are preserved in a stone chest: a depository for lives and deaths created in her mind and destroyed in her heart: a decimated organ, reconstructed time and time again with the force of her fingertips: the pulp of the greatest fruit torn apart by her conscience: servant to thoughts fallen from the sky: true bolts of light. Her bleeding, severed flesh turns into a mutable extract: her body can then assume new forms: there is hope that some emotions might morph into others: and yet, regardless of their appearance, hearts are in essence all the same: avatars of unpredictability. Brazen, Joan can perceive the complexity of what it is to be made from wind, devoid of preestablished paths: for all of these reasons, she holds within her huge potential: something akin to a thousand cataclysmic disasters trapped in a bottle. Music: to my disappointment, not the path she chose to pursue.

MAY

Ana

Cuckoo clocks and clocktower bells are the stuff of ghosts. Legend has it that spirits live inside both: the older the clocks are, the more entities they contain, since ghosts gravitate to their peals like magnets. My grandma was very old when she stopped ticking. Each day, a new piece broke. The spirits came to her, too.

Hollow, she made sounds on the hour, as though repeating words were her own particular chime. She'd been a person once, but now she was a cold, hard object propped against the wall. She forced us to remember our routine obligations, and every once in a while, she broke, her arms falling limp. It's very odd to imagine how a clock-person was once a person-person. That's how my mom would describe grandma when she talked about what she was like before, but I found it all hard to picture.

Maybe in an effort to convince me, my mom called me into her room and gave me a brooch shaped like a crown. My grandma-person had given her the brooch a long time ago. I accepted it, wondering how many years would pass before my own mom-mom would become an elder-clock. But before any of that, I'd have to adhere to the order of things, respect the responsibilities that come with age, have my own girl-daughter who would also inherit the brooch, as per this family tradition—but I was still young, and I still didn't know whether or not I'd ever grow something inside of me, let alone a new being that would hold my body hostage.

We'd visited grandma in the hospital a few days earlier. I never went into her room because I got distracted by a painting hanging in the hallway. It showed me what was to come, everything I needed to know: winged people rising upwards in a lilac spiral. The bodies became brighter as they ascended, their auras more powerful, their appearance more vigorous. Gold brushstrokes flecked the blue of the sky, creating spirals that carry these people to the realm of the dead, or so I deduced. On the other side of the canvas, figures walked on the ground with dirty feet, leaving well-defined footsteps in their wake. They wore masks made from a delicate material like porcelain that had small slits for their eyes and mouths. I imagined that they were afraid of breaking their masks, and that's what stopped them from braving the spiraled ascent.

A doctor in airy scrubs swished down the hallways between Gothic arches built from brick, or what looked like brick, my mom by his side. He interrupted my study of the painting to announce that grandma's condition was stable. The physician's bulletproof expression, his platitudes and tears, all indicated that the painting on the wall was a more reliable source of information.

The doctor's illusion gave us momentary relief fed by the feeling that believing him would make us suffer less, but his words were at war with the painter's brushstrokes. Maybe the artist painted the canvas on a happy summer afternoon, standing next to a big window in the hopes that they might be discovered as the next rising star in the art world, unaware of the role they'd play. A universe of possibilities, an entire existence deposited onto the surface of an object that would come to be displayed for people who found themselves in the intensive care unit of a hospital.

Joan

It was in the play of light and shadows that grandma saw a time of pain approaching. Every year as the seasons changed, we performed the same ritual: she took a bath infused with rosemary as the light of the reigning moon bounced off the surface of the water; she ate a fistful of raw chestnuts and breathed in the smoke from a bundle of smoldering herbs. Then she turned off all the lights in the house, stuffed cloth into the cracks beneath the doors, covered all the mirrors, and sat in her sculpted chair, murmuring a prayer I couldn't understand.

She closed her eyes and asked me to stand at a safe distance before moving a bright candle before her face. Only then did she ask me to come closer and spin the candle, to move it back and forth so that the dancing flame shifted in size. My grandma said that eyelids were like curtains; behind them, she could make out the truth of all things, freed from the disguises of their superficial appearance.

The little lick of fire created images that she could perceive in her mind's eye, located somewhere between the back of her eyeballs and the front edge of her brain. The flame carried information about events both near and far in the future, hopping between days, months, and years in vectors that ran in many directions and at different speeds. I never watched the images, focused as I was on carrying out the movements that my grandma announced, but I could sense the ballet that commanded the room where we stood, populating the walls with dancing figures. At those moments, we joined the flame and its shadows, the house and its revelations, tethered by an ancient art of divination.

After the ritual, we sat down together at the table for a light meal. I'd try to guess the discoveries by studying my grandmother's moods, the way she held her fork and knife, the tenor of her voice, and most especially the look in her eye as she gazed at me after that experience of momentary blindness to the outside world.

She didn't usually say much of anything about what she'd felt, heard, or seen, but in a subliminal language second nature to those in our bloodline, she shared what she learned. After all, my role wasn't just moving a candle. I created the patterns of shadow and light that communicated prophetic messages, and by using my body as a vehicle for that which stood beyond time but needed a body as a host to be understood, I honed my skills as a priestess.

Later that night, as visiting images still hung about the house, grandma spoke to me in an even tone and said that a woman very close to us, and maybe even more than one, would leave us very soon.

It was only a few months before that happened—or, rather, before something started to happen.

I'd been raised among the women of my family. Long before only grandma and I were left, we all got together on Sunday afternoons to talk about the goings on of the week, trade recipes, tell jokes and stories, confess, rant, spill whatever we needed to share. As time passed, I learned about their relationships, how they felt distant from their husbands. They were fun to be around even though the skins they'd wrapped themselves in were branded with hot iron.

It was hard to relish in the innocence of childhood and claim the name I'd chosen for myself in the midst of so many personal tragedies. The stories leeched into my flesh as a kind of collective pain, demanding recognition, no matter how belated.

I saw the full extent of the devastation in one of my relatives whose body had turned to skeletal dust. For years I felt the purge that ravaged our clan; I carry these women in my bones, with all their tattered clothes, their uncontrollable laughter, their disguises. Whenever I fail at something, my pain is immense, because I fail in my name and theirs. If I succeed, I've only done exactly what's necessary.

I always carry something more than what's contained in my limbs.

Grandma

I saw fragments and spheres, heard whispers and snippets of conversations. Everything that came to me – sounds, impressions, clipped images, emotions – arrived all at once in an agglutinated state in that place I'd never been to before but that I inhabited.

The scene was muddled, as though I'd submerged myself into some primordial cell of existence itself, deprived of my five senses, or at least of how they function in any other situation. I could grasp at fractions of greater truths, but without any of the resources that I'd typically use to decipher them. Back when I was younger, just about Joan's age, I found surrendering myself to this kind of divination difficult, but with practice I managed to understand how everything came to be and began to find my way. I learned to tame my fear before it tamed me. It came to stand by my side, passive as a dog that respects its owner each time I stepped into the narrow corridor between the back of my eyeballs and the edge of my brain.

I visited that liminal space because there, I was receptive to revelation. At times, I would see myself fully clothed, at others my body was bare, with only a veil cast over my shoulders. I have no control over my appearance in that place, just as I have no control over the images that emerge when Joan carries the flame.

Katarina, Joan's mother, gave me the girl at age six, telling me she wasn't ready for a child like that, one who decided to call herself Joan after learning what her given name signified to the world: the armor that would be placed on her back, the weapons and tools she would be handed, all inadequate supplies for a life growing in a different direction. I took her in, this girl of trees and moonlight, of cycles and omens, with the sense that she might give new life to whatever would die with me. Joan will follow me on my path, but she needs to command the external world before learning what it means to step into that darkness. She can enjoy herself in the theater of lights and shadows, think herself the master of a thrilling game, but on the inside, she'll have to step onto a floor of absence and death, the only space neutral enough for visions to appear uninhibited, and it can be terrifying.

One time, I revealed a piece of information that precipitated a period of hardship, pushing her out of the nest. She needed to know that childhood was behind her. Our tribe-family was made up of women who were neither heroes nor saints. They devoted themselves flesh and blood to their own survival; they suffered abuse in their relationships. Joan needed to understand them, to learn their language and codes, and to realize, most of all, that one day these women would cease to be.

In one of my visits to the hollow shell of future memories, I saw Joan's mother standing next to a much older woman. No matter how hard I tried to figure out who the woman was, her face was never more than a blur. Both wore rags and laughed and cried as they told me that they were trapped in their beliefs, that their blood flowed from a river, that full moons would be red and wreak havoc on the harvest. Katarina announced that her body parts were multiplying to the point that she would be un-recognizable. I saw versions of her with limbs out of place: arms hanging from her neck, veins spooling out from her skin, teeth speckling her hair, and bones growing on the outside of her body.

In the next image, the older woman was trapped in a structure that looked like a wooden crate. I could make out the shapes of her hands and her head behind the wood and hear her repeat words spoken by a masculine voice, also faceless.

Fire and ash enveloped the two women in the final image, and after murmurs and screams, they fell silent. A curtain opened; it was time to leave. Hours passed before I forced myself to speak with Joan and tell her, in the most natural way possible, that a time of pain was soon to reap incomprehensible fruits. A few months later, we learned that Katarina died from a disease that made her stomach bloat and leak. In the outpouring of fluids fleeing her body, her life, already stifled, slipped away. As for who the second woman was or what her fate held, at that point, I knew nothing.

JUNE

Ana

It's a known fact: men rule over the earth. They were granted the right to invade, fly, leap, and conquer. For women, on the other hand, expansiveness in body, mind, or action is distasteful, and we're declared insane or turned into sex objects by those same men who want so desperately to occupy our territories. The opposite of expanding is shrinking continuously, almost to the point of becoming invisible—a condition that might be worse than imprisonment, because at least in a cell, you have a floor and two feet that press firmly against it.

That's what I was thinking while smoking a cigarette that felt like a missile. I was standing with Rafael, Rosana Carvalho's son, and we balanced the slender sticks between our fingers, elegant as the mannequins in store windows. Our hands were flamboyant, softly illuminated by the coarse and crimson embers in the shadows. Our throats burned like the devil.

My eyes teared up every time the cigarette blazed, but I was getting used it. What a crazy thing, smoking: I felt like a fire-breathing dragon. As flames emptied into me, I soothed intimate ills. I pictured myself drying up inside, since my body isn't allowed to (1) spill outwards, (2) reassemble, (3) expand. Rafael, on the other hand, could simply let himself swell, everywhere or in just a few parts. We'd be perfect bibelots, fixed in place, anatomically unchanged. Put simply, we'd be young forever.

That afternoon, we walked around listening to indie rock. I relit my cigarette, a passport to the life I desperately wanted. Here's an observation: as much as we hate growing up, we never realize exactly when we became adults. We live in the contradiction of wanting to freeze bodies that are on fire. We refuse to accept the mutability of our bodies, but they change despite it all. I learned that lesson when I stepped on a neon green lizard that crossed my path. The creature was made from the latest laser technology, from intergalactic beams, and even though it was just a bit of gloop destined to be despised by humanity, it still chose to dart in front of me. When it comes to free will, we're the same, the lizard and me. Its body turned to liquid on the soles of my tennis shoes, the spitting image of the paint splotches used for party decorations but with the highest possible pigment quality. It was radiant in its mutant form, half dead, brilliant, debased at the penultimate stage of mankind's contempt.

On a scale from limitations imposed on bodies to full potential for expression, we're sometimes just a step beneath the lizard and the paltry rights the creature is guaranteed. Some people stand on the edge of the abyss, goaded onwards by an army of beliefs for which anything other than strict adherence is met with the threat of death. They end up in a state of limbo like shapeless ghosts, just white sheets with holes instead eyes. Changing bodies is met with so much hatred because it makes you realize how similar we are to those lizards: from one day to the next, we could turn to a sickening liquid and disappear.

Joan

There's an undiscovered goddess who has no name, legend, or myth. She isn't made from fire, air, water, or earth. Instead, she exists in between elements; she carries a bit of each and nothing of just one. Her domain is light passing through clouds, wind ripping through valleys, nights when the moon is blue, the buzz of bees, a beetle's beating wings, the pulse surrounding a fetus.

She understands an unspoken language made of gestures, intention, and intuition. She's either invisible or made of many colors, depending on how she'd like to remain unknown. Her laws and precepts shift based on needs—her own, and those of people who subconsciously appeal to her. Her altar is day and night, dawn and afternoon.

She emits fumes within her devotees, empties tides of ancient traumas and melodies carried by voices and oboes. She pulls arid lands from bodies as though they were treasure chests, opening space for a vegetable garden to be planted, eggs to multiply, and insects to land.

She's the fire that gave origin to waves, since oceans need a certain amount of heat to move. She teaches us that the air breathed by a community is conquered land, an instrument of power, as is the mood that colors the end of a long relationship shifting between silence and death. She carries tambourines of many sizes, all shaped like eyes, hanging from a belt around her hips.

Forever anonymous, she protects the non-binary, the mediums, the messengers, the wanderers. She's done so for more than half a century, long before her cult grew popular. Even still, her name, her real name, personal and unique, will never be known to anyone.

I become an itinerant explosion between electric shocks. An explosion in the form of a person. It's odd to define someone that way, but it's how I see myself. From the jolts that course through the body, pulling at fibers, muscles, nerves, and emotions, you can achieve illumination—only if you're open to finding it, of course. And some people reach illumination because of the mere fact that not many others are willing to do so, that's also true. I know I'm making a polemical point. I don't believe in villains or victims. What happens in this life are encounters, one person moving towards the next. Everyone learns from everyone else. I'm grateful to my torturer like I'm grateful to Swami. From the vantage point of the universe, everyone's enmeshed in the flux of things. If this happened to me, it means it was already written. I had to go through it. It was a form of liberation. The shocks freed me from a secular karma, see? I know, it's hard to grasp, I get it, really. Everyone has their moment. The time will come for all of us, there's no rush. Let go. Let it happen. I gave into the shocks. I released myself from my initial protests, and it was the best thing I could have done, because if I hadn't, I'd have never made my way to Swami. See? I saw energy in motion, lights refracting through me, and I became a cosmic spark. Humanness in its bodily form is so small compared to all that.

I gave myself the right to be free, so there's no one to forgive, only someone to thank for providing the seed, the earth. I am seed and earth, I grow in all directions, I feel the light, the currents coursing through me head to toe, pore to pore, to this day. I don't need anything else, since those forces live within me, present whenever I wish to access them. Isn't that a wondrous thing?

Love,
Rosana Carvalho

JULY

Ana

A militation of bodies. I came up with that word to describe the things I'd learned: mutation, mutilation, and the militancy of an activist. Having sex means touching spaces, fabrics, liquids, and residues as though they were jewels. Adoring parts of the body as though they were precious. Parts that society deplores but that are venerated for one miraculous moment. Then the feverish dance of bursting through physical boundaries ends, and bodies are shameful once again.

I performed a quick self-assessment and found images falling out of orbit. In a flash, they brought forward certain areas of my body and made hidden things clear. At the end of the day, women release our planet in clumps and shouts as it spins around each of us, constantly changing—and as we, in mutant form, turn along a single axis.

I don't want to be unexplored wilderness or an untouched forest, the ground where boots and tractors tread. I also don't want to be a force of nature and stoke the fetish of refusing purity, of breaking with the body. The guru once said: saints exist only to make the rest of humanity feel contemptable. From how I see it, forests and women have that same effect on men. That's why they're so set on subjugating us at all costs.

Good night! – Dona Suvyatic called out in a flat voice, opening the door to Mimi's room. This woman in her orange apron patterned with knitted turquoise flowers had breasts capable of storing the waters of an entire ocean. She was the captain of good manners, at least as it pertained to us two puerile beings who longed for the Internet, which, at least for us, wasn't a source of information, but instead a stairway straight to hell.

Thirty minutes earlier we'd watched videos in the following order: rocket-man invades boiler-woman; a scene between a painter and a homeowner who opened his garage door wearing a Speedo, a look of surprise passing across his face; schoolgirls in uniform, the pleats of their skirts shifting bawdily from side to side. I filed the images away as reference points in my imagination, in case later on I'd find myself less repulsed by such exercises of diluting the self.

It was like a rebirth. You shed money, pain, and barriers only to return a bit changed, with every indication that you won and lost in equal measure. The bedroom door opened; I flipped my notebook open while Mimi turned to face our mom, reciting the end of an essay about the Raggamuffin War that she made up on the spot. Unsure if we had any future at all, Dona Suvyatic left to check on her Slovakian cakes, which were still raw. Sitting in bed, Mimi unleashed a crazed giggle in total silence, as though she were trying to imitate those virile young girls on RoseTube.

At eleven forty-five that night, and without a dictionary on hand, I thought about how more than 97% of people couldn't tell the difference between the names of stars and venereal diseases, which both felt far removed and somehow close to my body and memory. From a distance, I'd already confused constellations of sounds and meanings: Denebola, Merope, Porrima, Chlamydia, Propus, Toliman, Donovanosis,

Errai, Gorgonea Tertia, Gacrux, Grumium, Condyloma Acuminatum, Regulus. A star bursting on the sky's nocturnal skin: blessing of blessings. A raised circumference on the flat expanse of the pelvis: a curse. I had a hard time understanding the laws that separated those events.

A wave of nausea and a specific kind of pain swept over me. I tried again and again to climb over the walls inside of me. My brain was shining, and my body obeyed from its roots, as though a machine of urges and instincts could trigger waves of red and heat. Triads accumulated across my territories. My throat expanded and my lips opened as I tried to sing ancestral melodies I knew by heart. Nervous that I'd get lost, I searched for Mimi. I needed her to mirror the fire: one body determining frequencies embedded in both. I was dunked in tanks of tepid water, submerging and resurfacing countless times. I could have died. I rushed into hair and skin: salamanders domesticated me, revealing the occult. I was whole, a fetus enveloped in sweet placenta, entranced earth. I ran the slippery path to meet her. Mimi declared our freedom. We'd reached the top. A tremor shook the ground beneath us. My lungs burned and I struggled to breathe.
    I couldn't sleep, and Mimi snored like an angel.

Dona Suvyatic

Waves crashed against my windows. I was in a house at the bottom of the ocean even though I lived in a city of identical homes built from brown brick, surrounded by a sparse forest. The massive body of water was outside each time the sky decided to fall.

Water plummeted and we cooked. Waves surged and we stirred soup.

Since we'd become residents of an air bubble immersed in those depths, we believed ourselves sheltered, at least temporarily, by a malleable, transparent, impassable film.

We cultivated warmth and affection in that peculiar seclusion. We spoke the language of fire and fed it kindling as if to make offerings to some beloved entity with faith that our food wouldn't turn out undercooked, raw, or burnt. I'd practiced the magic of creation ever since I was a child and carried my sisters with me since the day I was born. Some things are questions of fate in this life; others are fantasies that we wish were concrete. Back when there wasn't money for dolls, I made up imaginary friends. Later, when I didn't have a body that could bear children of my own, I found Mimi.

Removed from the infertility seen as an inescapable biological curse, I shouldered maternity for someone who couldn't carry her own child. The tears of a devastated, grateful woman pooled into a river at my feet. She sailed away on a boat without the bundle she once held.

A new life in my arms, I didn't dare open the windows out of the fear that water might flood in. There were two of us now. Mimi was surrounded by the elements that would either swaddle us or swallow us whole. But if we kept the water outside, we'd just stay huddled there, and that seemed like it would be enough. We lived inside, our faces and clothes yellowing from the reflection of the fire, our eyes shifting colors depending on the strength of our domestic flame. Waves crashed, but we ignored their call.

Mimi grew up. Years slid by and the hearth no longer had everything we needed. My daughter's movements grew in strength and size: with a flick of her wrist, the kettles would fly; with one simple sigh the bread wouldn't rise; with a single complaint all of my sewing would come undone.

We needed to move, if only to make sure we had space, continuity. I wanted to work, and Mimi needed to go to school. That was the time of the great flood. After pressing down on us for years, the water broke through our barriers, crashing through windows, walls, and doors, destroying more than what a fire could burn. Only the dust of our past lives remained. Our tears dried up, and Mimi and I set off for new lands in a vehicle that traveled on air.

It's been a few years since we moved here. Now we have a floor and rooms to fill with the promise of permanence. There's no water waiting for us outside. She studies, I work. Our eyes sometimes dart between gas stovetops and their ignitors. Out of sight, there are stars and bugs, airplanes and helicopters, and electric powerlines that crisscross against the sky.

Joan

11:34 PM

The planet fell asleep red. Then came the taste of death: a com-
bination of fear, pain, and surprise dissolving across the tongue.
I wanted to hold him in my arms, but I knew that standing stiff
and immovable by his side was the greatest act of generosity
for a man from his generation who'd valued pride above all else
from the moment he was born. To be consoled by an emotional
woman would be of no help at all; to the contrary, it would just
make him feel indulgent. I intuited this. My heart was beating
hard, and I hoped that Uncle Oscar wouldn't notice my chest
heaving with every thud.

*Experts recommend changing your sleeping position if thoughts
torment you when you go to bed, or if memories drift through your
mind like floating waste. Not a very effective strategy, I'd say.*

11:45 PM

I squashed a bug on the wall. It wasn't meant to be there. I
felt remorse for its death and for my heavy hand, so implacable
and uncritical. Which hand decides the fate of human beings?
Time doesn't move on its own. There must be someone out
there, some other equally devastating force.

11:57 PM

As I visited a series of places in the effort to recuperate experiences or a piece of who I was, everything felt new yet already
traversed: I related to things and people as though for a second
first time. Is it time that escapes us, or is it the ground beneath
our feet? We've all fled a part of ourselves that will never return,
but that once in a while insists on determining our futures and
our dreams.

*The cold body in our bed might even be acceptable if we knew what
its presence meant all along. In that case, he serves us, not the other
way around.*

12:12 AM

I wanted to have a heart-shaped greenhouse filled with plants.
Not because I wanted to make an emotional appeal, or worse,
an appeal to insecurities; no, a greenhouse and the human
heart are symbols of total comfort and extreme disorder. Plus,
red and green go so well together. Imagine: a strawberry-fruit
and a jade-stone lying side by side.

*The frigid body in your bed can be a collaborator, even an old friend
who draws your attention to the poetry of passing years, assuming
there's a mutual understanding. You won't sleep a wink, but you'll*

be more creative. Cohabitation will enhance an artistic talent bur-
ied within you, if you haven't already dedicated yourself to one.

12:26 AM
− What city are you trying to find?
− A city that doesn't exist anymore, a frequency without vibrations, one that acts on the sensory nervous system through
  mental images. I feed on the ghosts of these cities, which is
  a bit depressing.

If you're concerned that the cold presence will produce thoughts of
flesh and song over the course of more than eight hundred paradisi-
cal dreams, there are mind-drawings and a hidden language that
can protect you. Stay alert, and never, ever give in to him completely.

12:37 AM
Some claim to have discovered their lifelong vocation as children. That's a phenomenon we might describe as "the body of
a child cloaked in a costume of total certainty." In other words,
it's the negation of the essential dynamism of existence, a condition that could kill you or leave you in a coma.

Memory is an underground train that follows us from birth. The
cold body is nothing more than a slave to Memory. And She forces
him to be her messenger, carrying scenes trapped in the basement
of the past, present, and future. Those memories can bring us to the
brink of insanity or into a state of extreme intolerance for the self
and others, if received without the necessary preparations.

12:42 AM

Baking a cake is not unlike sacrificing a body to a demon during a séance. You have to follow instructions. Cleanliness, invocation, evocation, magic words, protective measures, the selection and separation of ingredients, energy ushered in, preparation of the space and the utensils. Smoke, whispers, shapes, instruments. Growth, heat, careful timing, full materialization, a feast, and the final sacralization of the food.

Coming full circle, the apparition leaves once the messages of Memory are transmitted. The bed feels spacious. If the memories were honored by the person who received them, noises filter in along with comforting, symbolic images, and she'll wake up wiser than when she lay down.

12:59 AM

Red rain fell. It left me livid, surrounded by a bloody downpour. I climbed mountains inside of myself, and my eyelids grew heavy as I lost oxygen. Little by little, my thoughts slipped away. Sleep finally came to me when I was a mere two steps from the summit, the edge of the abyss. Alone, I finally saw him: king of dreams.

AUGUST

Ana

My dad kept a stack of heavy books above his tall dresser in the way that people hide guns, chocolate, and cigarettes. He relished the thought that someone wouldn't be able to resist the urge to flip through the pages of a distant epoch and discover those almost-inaccessible treasures—treasures that make a real difference in our flat little lives, once they're revealed. The ladder was always there. Or the stepping stool. Or whatever else was needed to support the reader in their ascent.

I managed to grab the biggest volume, a hardcover photo album containing one-of-a-kind images mixing photography and ink. Bookworm larvae and portraits riddled pages coated in plastic, untouchable in that particular way dead relatives always are.

An Eastern Orthodox priest caught my eye among the many faces. He had a white beard and a black hat and wore a crucifix, which hung from a thick cord around his neck. His gaze, rigid and insistent as the law and symbolism of the wooden cross, combined realism and a touch of the fantastical. A tour guide of sorts, the priest started to tell a story, his voice loud and clear, as though I were wearing headphones.

Father

Entering the priesthood was the great paradox of my life. A soul like mine should never have been shut inside an ordinary tomb of normative rules, where beliefs had no hope of escape. And yet, as someone caught between the chill of winter, the heavens, and the rosary, the Church's robes served me well.

I was somewhere between martyrdom and inexistence, between obligations of marriage and devotion to God, charting a third path that felt removed from who I was. I surrendered to prayer and benevolence, leaning into to the sumptuousness with which the pious are protected. I sought out the strange: I extended an outstretched arm to the enemies of order and common sense, to the marginalized, the unique, the perverted. In me, they were able to find support and certainty, and this linked me to the foundations of a Christian faith.

Subject as they were to injustice since the times that creed had no language, women became my confidants. I spoke to them on nights when candles burned end to end, from one shift to another, throughout a vigil. Truth can be found in words that form in between prayers: these are revelations in their greatest expression.

I wasn't born at an ideal moment for experiencing the things I dreamed about. It was as though my spirit had made a mistake when selecting the moment in which to be born, when choosing an epoch that would allow it to blossom, to open possibilities for existence, to exteriorize the self.

My only option—save planning a premature death—was to make do with what had been given to me by some higher power. It wasn't in my character to pass judgement. In an effort to alleviate the imprisonment with which I was born, I did what I could to liberate others from their own prisons, or to help them feel free for a few hours.

I unleashed my vices and brought my ideas of freedom and rebellion to the few teachers and superiors I trusted. I was naïve. I was persecuted, captured, and then doubly imprisoned.

I never stopped supporting others as they protested, not even in a forced labor camp. I knew equality would be the result of furious and highly conscious acts.

Months passed before my body was executed by the knife held by a young man who often visited my cell. We'd acted in secret, but my freedom, relative as it was, had vibrated at a frequency that abandons, blinds, and destroys.

That night, I covered my bare body with a red gown of Chinese silk, passed down from my mother to me.

Ana

As I heard the story behind that almost mythic figure, I realized how a flimsy old image had the power to shake me. It's no coincidence that some indigenous groups believe that pictures can imprison the spirit of the person being photographed.

I reached the top branches of my family tree only to realize that I didn't lead a life of revolutions. I'd climbed a rusty ladder just to come to the conclusion that you shouldn't mess with the dead or with mountaintops, not unless you're performing witchcraft or if there's truly nothing else to do. I resonated with the second motive, which was at least moderately respectable. I'd wanted to dig through the archeology of my family history, to reveal the actions of those who'd given rise to my features, to the heads of my waters.

Closer now to a narrative that could save my generation, I could understand what made for a good story of life and death. As I turned towards the past, I faced what it might mean to build a respectable life.

The late spring weather was unstable. The sound of someone shouting goodbye and the kaboom of a thousand metal cans clanging hung in the air. I was perched at the top of the ladder, caught between the chill of winter, a rose bush, and the heavens. A clap of thunder, then a rolling blackout across the city. I saw the connections, and the pyrotechnic flashes of one lightning bolt after another were more than enough to show me the way.

I fell, twisting my ankle from all the weight I'd been carrying. I'd end up walking more forcefully, a little stronger in my stance, but also more slowly. I accepted my fate, wayward steps and all. There was no going back: I'd learned about the pain that the world holds, and all of the worlds contained in a single moment of pain. I had to continue onwards. Before, I'd just been walking in circles.

Joan

The last time I met the lady in the tree she told me a fable. In a faraway time and place, there was a community of cat-people so dissatisfied with the differences that separate humans and beasts that they leapt over the bounds of biology and rational thought in order to behave like cats.

For around five hours each day, these people practiced what they called "cat-isms": they lifted their tailbones towards the moon while lapping cream from fine chinaware; they meowed in a chorus of tones and practiced their purrs, which weren't all that convincing; they frequented polemical lectures on the subject of The Art of Becoming a Feline-Human-Citizen or How to Live Well as a Soul Separated from the Body. Laudable efforts, no doubt about it; the more difficult the exercise, the greater respect it would garner.

Donning clothes made from artificial fibers, they licked themselves and their fellow felines, swallowing fine threads that were ill-suited to the human digestive system. To facilitate the purge of residual matter that clung to the inner walls of their intestines, they imbibed bitter laxatives, and right away their bodies expelled turbid waters as their abdomens contorted in cramps that felt never-ending, in the way stomach pain always seems to feel.

They were sad and they were happy, those beings desperate to forget their original forms, who wanted to be something other than what they were, who searched for outer casings better suited to their spirits.

Human beings live in an extended attempt to occupy other bodies. That's the source behind the dream of private property, expensive clothes, powerful animals—the unrestricted accumulation of goods to envelop delicate skin. It's the need to feel like an egg yolk, surrounded by layers of matter that protect from friction with the stuff of the universe. Man hides from man who hides from man in successive symbolic layers, like nesting dolls deprived of all purpose.

With endless curiosity and limitless territory to explore, members of the community constructed paths with perches, landings, and tunnels in fortuitous places. In the minds of the bipedal cats, bodies had no fixed meaning, not for thinking, nor for words, nor for using objects. Everything could change at any moment, whenever one hand of the clock moved away from the other.

However, as one would expect from the universal law of birth-growth-procreation-death, the desire to adhere to the practices of cat-isms faded after about a decade. This was the simple cause of the low membership retention rate in that artificial tribe with its organic airs.

At one point, the community counted over one hundred thousand members. Years later, it hovered around a thousand. In the last census, a mere fifty. The fur suits were sold at a discount in second-hand shops, and there aren't any records of collectors or fetishists taking any interest in the items.

Undiscovered Goddess

Despite their rootedness in legends and unbridled obsession with bodies, the cat-people were the opposite of urban vampires in the twenty-first century.

Each vampire possessed three billion books archived in their bodies. Every language known to mankind, dead, living, or wounded, was housed along the tops of their tongues, almost touching their upper canines, which were sometimes natural, sometimes prosthetic.

Truth be told, they've always fought to keep being vampires. They revere their natural state and possess an enviable sense of self-esteem. I've never met one who's humble.

For vampires, everything is about respect for the histories they carry. Forget about blood, glamor, goblets, velvet, castles, stiff collars, or rings—a single vampire is much more akin to a new edition of the complete works of the Library of Alexandria.

Blood is just the ink with which they absorb that corpus in its entirety. A vampire is the enviable sum of darkness. An inflatable doll made of steel. A being that cannot be recycled. That can never catch fire.

If you happen to see a vampire tremble with pleasure as it swallows a gulp of blood, don't be fooled: that's a reaction to the stories that occupy its body. A vampire is pure nostalgia enhanced by advanced technology. A vampire is a non-body, filled with certainty, collectivity, elegance, and precision.

SEPTEMBER

Ana

He was red all over, that's what he was, from his hair to his bashful disposition. Like a catalyst for a specific visual frequency, he absorbed everything around him that was ruby in tone. Some people go about stealing what belongs to others—and then there I was, aware of him in his entirety. I couldn't stop watching him.

At twenty, he walked alongside his mother-maybe-stepmother, Olga Veiga's granddaughter, at the dawn of her forty-seventh adolescence. She searched in the folds of her skirt—or in the wind her skirt produced as she twirled before the mirror—for a physical condition that no longer existed.

We carry around dead pieces of our bodies that we pretend are still alive. Botox, face lifts, acid peels, and laser treatments are all evidence to my point. They help us forget our depleted skin, our failing muscles, our unused cellulite.

That's not to mention new technology promoting "physical permanence, forever unchanging," acquired with an exclusive trademark by Seven Spheres. There, at that clinic frequented by the hyper-wealthy, people ingest seven types of nutrients each day with the goal of losing seven kilos per week—and, over the course of the treatment, rejuvenate themselves by the measure of seven years, seven months, and (of course) seven days.

Like a sun rising over costumes in a women's clothing shop, the boy with his mop of red hair seemed to have been born with the sole purpose of drawing sharp contrast between the ideal of youth and the woman who stood by his side.

Half artificial, half organic, I might even dance with him, however cool and tepid and well on my way to that deliberate death that hits us as the age of twenty-eight. A hint of respect is merited by those who occupy an intermediary zone, or so the rules say.

Those who put themselves in that post-youthful zone are seen as the stuff inside a coffin at progressive stages of decay. Bring on the judgments, the specialists' evaluations!

I'll kiss him before my time comes, my lips bursting with filler, and try to get closer to the innate power of a man-child that lasts fifty-four years. Some consider this delayed maturity to be charming. They say men frozen in time are the result of mother nature, this stunted growth a thing blessed by divine providence.

Maybe the ruby-red boy could love me with his hyper-saturated vermillion heart accumulating pigments. He'd probably want to marry me, to consume me, to ignore me, to see me as flesh, absent only the blue rubber stamp confirming my quality and provenance. On the bright side, I wouldn't be alone.

I'd love him and no one would ever doubt it, at least not over the course of that afternoon, as I tried things on in the dressing room and sheaths of fabric cut through moments of eye contact as we moved between mirrors and pouffes, which were as decorative as the store's headless mannequins—ideal and immobile silhouettes deprived of brains and speech. That afternoon, I picked out a dress for my eighteenth birthday.

The dress was baby blue for a time in life when babies are undesirable. Coherence isn't worth much for those with the audacity to be woman and child all at once. I let myself open out beneath layers of ruffles, proving that something else exists in the interior of my interior of my interior: each woman is infinite in her derivative selves, a Russian doll regardless of whether she's Slavic, Brazilian, Arab, or imaginary.

Different types of trimmings circumscribe each stage of existence. Hemmed with fine fabric on the outside, the borders are memorable, dignified, pleasant. On the inside, crafted from desire, anticipation, and nightmares, they're repulsive, degrading, dirty, though this is what determines our shape, inside and out. That's the curse we perpetuate, us dolls, who primp our passing days.

Truth lies in a seed somewhere in the depths of me. A seed of terrifying sensations—so I told myself—the kind that could shake the cosmos if tended carefully.

These thoughts passed through my mind as I crossed the street with my mom, caught under the gaze of seamstresses specialized in rites of passage: baptisms, fifteenth birthdays, eighteenth birthdays, engagements, weddings, marriages I, II, III, and IV, and burials.

Joan

To love is to fill one lung with suffering and the other with stones. A belly full of otters, a leg of lamas, rump like a basket of gold that could fit a calf or whole human child. It's playing jump rope with an unpredictable whip, dancing as though the day begins and ends with the rhythm of your feet; it's a trickle that turns into a river, a waterfall, an ocean current; it's applause that begins before the show comes on stage, subverting the order of things. It's red earth that sweats from sprouting so many seeds, a beating sun that pushes the edges of the earth in every direction. To love is to open space for little stoves across the body, making room for egalitarian occupations; it's deciphering the language of snakes at the moment they hisssss, carving space in your chest for a heart, maybe two.

On the position the body adopts when it's filled with multiple souls: take note if one side or the other stays suspended in excess, if gestures become overly theatrical or all too perfect; this is a thing that signals pride, a planned performance, or a deep need to be watched, which runs counter to the nebulous movements of a ritualistic trance that begins when spirits take over our limbs and dance in their particular way.

It happens when we realize that we're blindly navigating an ocean, trusting that someone in the heavens or on earth will guide our path and watch over our survival until we reach shore and step onto firm sand once again.

The utmost attention to each of these details is highly recommended. To love—or to surrender, to believe—also requires a healthy dose of skepticism.

Grandma

Fists pounded against the door. On the second to last knock, a policeman announced himself, holding what he claimed to be a search warrant allowing him to inspect every home in the area. There was a security concern; rumors were circulating that fugitives had hidden somewhere in the neighborhood.

He walked inside and searched my pots and pans, asking me who I lived with, where Joan's real mother was, how we managed to get by. I told him about the herbal medicines and food we made to order, explained how everything came from the plants in our garden except for goods we traded in the community. He listened while opening lids of jars, sniffing the essence of our potions and spices with avid curiosity.

Before leaving, he turned back to ask one last question.

We don't keep Bibles in this house, I answered.

Recife, September 7th

Being in the struggle means having a roar in your teeth, in the soles of your feet, in the parts of you that sweat. You need your good hand ready to reach for a knife, to hold a rifle, to shoot a revolver, to recall the longitude and latitude of a shotgun. And that's not all.

They always said I had a knack for doing several things at once without losing focus. That's what I put into practice in the soft palate of the dark forest, deep inside the mouth of trees, surrounded by the high-pitched whine of an unknown power.

I was told to place my finger on the trigger (light pressure only, so as not to shoot in vain), to trick the stomach out of grumbling by chewing sap siphoned from the ground, to guess the size of the slug that had made my right leg its home, to deduce how many steps I'd be able to take without leaving a trace, to imagine what my comrade in arms was thinking two leagues away while moonlight multiplied through the leaves overhead.

Being in the struggle isn't just following the trace of the enemy's slaughter. It's sight and stillness in an intensity I'll never feel again.

Write down the things I'm telling you.

Um abraço,
Olga Veiga

OCTOBER

Ana

Right after stepping out of the shower, I heard a voice coming from the mirror while I was still surrounded by steam. The words were clear as a sonnet emerging from the depths of the sea. In fact, they were suspended between the layers of silver and glass used to compose a more-than-perfect reflection, hidden within one of those inventions created by men who play God, as though the creator had wished to invent a universe in duplicate.

It said:

. . . river dams ruptured, causing criminal catastrophes. Just think—buried animals,

dirt-filled screams catching in throats, unskilled bodies trapped, capsized boats, thick boils that form a shuddering pain, darkness unleashed, faith disappearing, the mud, the earth, the bedrock accumulating in layers that were never meant to form.

. . . one hundred and eleven rounds fired; five boys dead. Just think—five hearts filleted, halted refrains, agile fingers snapping in the slow five minutes before shots rang out, a young person's refusal to believe in death, the rogue escape of a white car riddled with bullet holes.

. . . the things that reduced Dandara, the travesti, to human garbage. Just think—a body kicked and crushed, a chewed up, spit out nerve, rotting flesh you try to avoid, a wound that hurts like hell,

that you'd set on fire. A body ground to bits, pulverized, broken, polluted, tortured by men who see femininity as lesser, impure, tempting—something to be negated with the most extreme measures.

. . . the thirteen bullets that took Marielle. Just think: a car scarred by bullets, the body of a mother bleeding out, wrestled out of history, a river that will never again see waters running high, wife and daughter caught in rigid flames, secular power contained in one short life, a lighthouse to so many. An era to rediscover, to reconstruct; defeat.

. . . a routine police search over Luana Barbosa's butch body. Just think: the beating, five days in the hospital, her job, blunt trauma, the skull, the bullet, a game of billiards, the girl, a battered body, her son, the back of a police vehicle, the "no, sir," or the "no fucking way," the end.

. . . hundreds of millions dead in a pandemic left ungoverned, in a country that has ceased to exist.

Joan

I started feeding myself on memories of places, like the basement of a music conservatory in a mansion from the early
1800s. I studied the cello there, in a setting that promised me
a career as a musician. I dropped out after a few months (I'd
mostly been motivated by Uncle Oscar).

The fact that I can remember the floorplan of that building says a lot about my ability to internalize spaces and the
things they carry with them. That home of study and reclusion
gave me comfort at a time when uncertain futures were something to be desired.

At the end of the day, one needs intelligence and versatil-
ity in equal measure to navigate the detours and chance events
of an artistic life, a sea that can't tolerate a static ship, which is
a quality I've always found compelling.

It was different, this time. I had to reconstruct a home
that would one day serve me; it wasn't just a memory, but it also
didn't belong to the present moment.

Grandma had been taken by the authorities, and she'd be
questioned soon, subject to an investigation into her practices
of art and sleep, provisions and resistance, which were recently
banned by the state. As the one left behind, I felt exposed; I
needed to hide my flora, my nakedness, the things others saw
as unacceptable.

The house had been a living organism when grandma was there; without her, I swayed between four wooden sticks rising from unstable ground.

I thought about the questions they'd ask and whether metal stakes and electric currents snaked around her body.

A story was circulating in the neighborhood: women were being turned to ash in "public bonfires," a perverse witchcraft practiced by men who claimed to be religious.

Waiting this out wasn't an option. With repression spreading like flames in a dry forest, I needed to act. I mustered the courage I'd need to use everything I learned. Maybe it wasn't the right time, maybe grandma would have told me to wait a few more years, but this was a moment driven by necessity, not desire.

I drew a bath infused with rosemary as reflections of the moon above appeared in the water, white and full of new omens. The stretch of time between the moment in which I'd started chewing nuts and my first sniff of smoke from smudged herbs lasted ten slow blinks. Objects around me disappeared and reappeared, first enveloped in sunlight, then covered in shadow.

Inside, I'd already draped all the mirrors and objects made of silver or aluminum with long skirts, sheets, flags, and towels embroidered with the royal insignia of our unrecognized clan.

As I sat on the sculpted throne, I came into contact with history, transmitted to my body with each passing step.

I reached for a candle. Grandma had already used it, and I needed that symbolic comfort, the belief that this object made of wax and paraffin could give rise to a flame filled with revelation.

If everything went according to plan, I'd be the one to both orchestrate the movement of the fire and receive the messages. That was no easy task, since I'd need to rely on intuition and act as two people.

Beyond the possibility of losing myself forever in the space between the backs of my eyes and the edge of my brain, I had no clue of what might happen. If I were to get lost, I'd go blind, alone without anyone to help me move forward—but no ledge is too high for someone who's already on the ground.

I took a deep breath and closed my eyes as I held the candle in front of me, moving the flame as gracefully as possible. I saw the flush of red on the backs of my eyelids that marked an entrance into prophetic vision.

I was afraid that I'd enter an intense trance and lose the focus I needed to move the candle. My hand should never stop moving. Visions form from the sway of the flame against negative space, flame against negative space.

As I'd intended, I moved towards the back of my head to visit the unexplored depths behind the shallow, fatalistic thoughts that were front of mind. I needed to surrender, have faith, and wield skill and restraint in equal measure to not fall prey to waves of illusions and mistaken impressions, which could make me lose everything.

I reached the zone of future memories: a warehouse for all that is to come. A place that doesn't obey the idea of linear time, which is such a useful resource for structuring our egos in everyday life. In that zone, a circle cuts through the waters to frame a space filed with florescent mist, an auspicious setting for predictions.

I thought about grandma, how I wanted answers about her whereabouts. Five days had passed since she'd given me her blessing, five days I'd been without roots, embrace, or enrichment.

The circle grew dark. Maybe it was nighttime in whatever abysmal place she was being held. But no, it was a place without windows, with dull lamps at various points around the enclosure. I heard a cough from lungs filled with stagnant water and followed the sound to a vision of grandma.

In a hold that appeared to be inside a large wooden crate, grandma stood facing me, opening and closing her eyes as though in a trance, either on the threshold of death or at the brink of the greatest revelation of the century. But she was simply exhausted and dispirited. Putting bodies through hell is the only way to punish those who don't believe in an afterlife, and her torturers were well aware of that fact.

I saw a series of images repeated in quick succession: the cross, an altar, a bonfire, feet running through the forest, my face, the cross, an altar, a bonfire, feet running through the forest, my face. They flooded towards me, and I understood that words were being repeated by a single torturer. He asked her the same questions countless times.

Grandma answered again and again until she had no languages left to think in, no thought left to say, her body disobeying every command as it failed to recognize logic behind which actions her speech might provoke.

I needed to know who that man was, and I'd empty out every building in the city to find the cell.

Suddenly, my body grew hot, as though I were inside one of the earth's layers buried deep underneath the ocean, where lava heats the world's waters. Drifting from the hollow zone of future memories, I turned my attention back to the candle and opened my eyes. Melted wax covered my lap; my dress was scorched. The back of my right hand was encased by the dry shell of once-molten heat.

The house was dark. It took me a minute to figure out if I'd reached the twilight of my vision or if it was just dark outside. I moved slowly, groping at furniture until I reached the window, where I could see the fresh moon in the sky. For the first time, I'd experienced revelations, but there was nothing to celebrate. Like a branch severed from its tree, I'd lost my roots and approached a premature end while slowly dripping sap.

Suddenly, I felt an intense need to free myself of my burnt clothing. I pulled a green dress from the trunk, the only piece of fabric I could find. I had no idea that I'd wear it one other time, on the night of my eighteenth birthday.

NOVEMBER

Ana

My teeth ripped at flesh. First, I tore open an outer layer, but that didn't satisfy my rush of desire, so I bit and gnawed until I reached the innermost section marked by the limit of pain and the whitish glimpse of bone.

Filled with power and destruction, my actions unleashed a gush of blood and some kind of meaning. I was trying to defeat my enemy.

I rolled across the fuzzy brown rug, my short hair mixing with synthetic fibers like it was possible to create a union between elements of contrasting composition. I ignored the words blasting from the television, even though I could hear them perfectly. My brother pulled at my hair, then dove to bite my shoulder; I felt him land on top of me, full of muscle and will, but there was no chance he'd win: the floor was my territory. It gave me the strength to stand during the few seconds we weren't in combat.

The TV shouted again, trying to trade hearts for products. I fought for my native land, for hair, which was the greatest of contradictions in the aesthetic values of our current moment.

Oswald had only a bit of stubble scattered across his body, and that's obviously why he hated my hair. He wanted to be respectable, while I displayed my savagery for him and everyone else to see.

It all started with a shaving cream commercial. People always find a way to develop products like those white, mass-produced puffs of purity and hygiene, which get rid of the things they find undesirable.

Disgusting, obscene, hairy, vile masc hairy girl, my brother shouted, which only goaded me on. A hysterical spectator to human drama, the television continued emitting random phrases, which mixed with Oswaldo's insults to form a new, incomprehensible language.

Joan

If a fly were looking out my window, the perpendicular lines of a building splitting the darkness of the sky would serve as proof that the earth is flat. A similar explanation would suffice for the man-fly. The fly and its kin, the man-fly, differ only when it comes to their physical appearance—the sedimentation of their outer matter and nothing more. Their eyes and mentalities are exceedingly similar, especially when it comes to seeing and comprehending the things around them.

I was whole and spheric and filled with layers, roots, antennae, and scales—that is, I was the way I'd always seen myself. The dim lights flickering around the house seemed to multiply, as though thousands of lives contained in the body of a woman approaching her eighteenth birthday refracted against the walls.

This time I was less nervous during preparations and even at the moment I achieved the conditions favorable to accessing visions. In addition to the ceremonial steps of chewing nuts, draping fabrics to prevent reflections, smelling the essence of herbs, and taking a bath beneath the reigning moon, I swallowed the bitter, earthy drink that made me rock back and forth. Filled with vertigo, I stopped at the moment of about-to-move-forward, not the point of return.

There, I'd no longer run the risk of leaving the hollow zone of future memories if I didn't want to, which would allow me to surrender even more. I wanted clear visions without interruption.

I held the candle, sure that this time, the movements would guide my hand, not the other way around.

Fluctuating in the dark depth of my own eyes, neither separate from nor ignorant of the spinning motions, I felt the moment arrive.

The Lady in the Tree

My parrot brings me information. He's my messenger, and I need him. He has the wings my body lacks, the colors I've always searched for. I emulate them with clothing and hats, sometimes with scarves or sweet drinks.

The parrot is my tropical soul. And you, Joan, are lovely. Your grandma trained you well. If you continue down this path, you'll be one of the few to carry on a practice of receiving visions in that space you've named the hollow zone of future memories.

I'm pleased you called on me. I'm the liquid you drank and the thing that is beyond. I live in the tree at the summit, waiting for answers from the parrot. You and I share a kind of closeness, which is rare. I can't be captured, which is lucky. They just keep taking people, just as they took your grandmother.

Men who come knocking on your door with questions never have good intentions. If they stick their noses in pans and rummage through pots and traditions, their intentions are worse still. If they ask why there's no crucifix hanging from the walls, it's best to leave before they return—because they will return, and they've filled many cells with women, old, young, and middle-aged.

See, the exit might be blocked, but an exit always exists, even if the lock on the crate never opens. There's another kind of hope for escape and freedom, especially for your grandmother. She's already started practicing the techniques. Even though she knows nothing of prisons, she's well versed in rebellion.

I believe she'll resist—that the lock will be opened, her torturer annihilated. But she must reach an auspicious state for that to occur. She's overcome apathy, and now she practices her magic. Light doses, but she's already getting results. She could make a nail fall from the wall just by looking at it, visualizing it. Matter is the mother of us all, and it's profoundly capable of being influenced, depending on what we whisper in its ear. If we want to tell her something, we must act like her daughters, or so the parrot says.

I'm very proud of you Joan. Now, I'll make space for the next.

Undiscovered Goddess

Like men, flies aren't very good at anything. The similarity has nothing to do with an ability to fly but instead to idolize waste and hold it as the reference point for appearing respectable. A man can produce the sound that a fly's wings make with his tongue, which shouldn't be a point of pride.

But they are proud of (1) propagating destructive noises, and (2) transporting pieces of feces with their feet and hiding them across the four corners of the planet's body as though dung were treasure.

I don't command anyone, but I do have the power to guide the flies, to ask that they visit certain orifices and plant their eggs of destruction.

From eggs appear tiny larvae capable of decimating huge lives; they chew long bodies millimeter by millimeter in an infinitesimal marking of time. The way in which larvae and flies keep time is radically different from that of the human species: they make a single hour seem gigantic.

Some men crave destruction and for that reason keep women cloistered. His desire to capture her justifies his drive to possess natural resources. She is too full of surprises to be acceptable in a precise system, contained in the pages of a book that will never enjoy a second print run.

I've asked the flies to visit the orifices of the torturer who took your grandmother. In three moons, he'll suffer from fluids and itches, Satan's warts and exposed flesh. All the while, the woman in the box, with her flexibility of mind, will alter full paragraphs in the book of unchangeable ideas. Words well-said can change reality. I always work with that aim, waiting for the day I'll be discovered. That will only happen when the moon changes color and descends towards Earth.

This is everything I can reveal. Now, I surrender my place to someone more important.

Grandma

It can be hard to form words from thoughts because a unique bodily mechanic reigns over the mind. The time has come to put into practice what I've learned, because otherwise, dedicating myself to study for so many years wouldn't make any sense at all.

Joan, what does it mean that you performed the ritual of lights and shadows alone, that you lost your need for entertainment, making way for immersion and focus? I understand that you're afraid, but we never think ourselves ready until that's the only option.

We find ourselves in similar circumstances. I've dedicated myself to this, just as you have. I move about half-awake; you, in the depths of depths. The hallucinations tied to visions are a slow dive into parts of us that are banned. Among other things, the visions help us slip past fear. Let them happen. Twisted paths lead to precise revelations.

To rave delirious is to suffer pathologies and excuse them with fantasies. Or it's to have fantasies and excuse them with pathologies. It's to be torn apart while the soul stays intact and alert. The lady in the tree and the undiscovered goddess use those pathways to access your consciousness, just as I'm doing now.

Don't be distressed by the crate and my confinement. They can't tie anything down except for this old body. Everything else can escape—including a body, depending on the technique and control of those who practice a certain kind of magic. You should know that we entered the mind of the man who arrested me days ago. And you must know that I don't walk alone. The lady in the tree and the undiscovered goddess helped me plant two, three, many intruders into the mental field of my torturer. They take on many sizes, and they command him. Of everyone here, he's the only person who's been dominated.

The intruders appear to be friends, but they demand his constant attention, threatening and caressing him and constantly causing conflict. The torturer is made of smoke and moves according to the air's commands; he is never present in the reality that pursues him, neither in body nor mind. Mentally, it's hard to put up resistance in such a position.

The Torturer

I'm never alone. The others, nebulous as they are, never leave my side.

Here, underground, there's the fly, the clown, Verigna, the dog, and the rat.

When the fly flies, I hear the laughter of a thousand babies in diapers.

It buzzes towards and away from me in quick, erratic movements. It grows as big as a mountain, then shrinks to the size of a coffee bean.

The clown is green and black and spins on his heels in place. He utters phrases in a language I barely understand, growling, neighing, and uttering lascivious innuendos until his inflamed lips open wide and tall flames rise from his head.

Verigna is a girl; she came from a pit full of stones and coal. She scratches at me with a knife, hunting for liquids—semen, pus, ointments, saliva, brine, or sweat. She threatens to cut my face, then swears she loves me while saying that I need to be dominated, that I should have scars.

Then there's the dog that looks like a bear. He's the only one I think of as a friend. He's as large as a tall man and innocent, like a child who refused to grow up. He eats cotton candy in bright colors and then burps. He asks me if I want to go to the park with him, but every time I accept his invitation, a vortex leading to the center of a foul-smelling swamp appears in front of me, and I shrink away.

Twenty-four is a number, and it's also the rat. He scurries around, ordering me to begin the beatings—with a hammer, my hand, scissors, whatever's in front of me. Beat a child, a mother, a doctor, an old woman, the dog, whoever's in front of me. I don't have scissors or a hammer, just hands and keys. But that's what he tells me, so I make do with what I have, which is someone to hit.

DECEMBER

Tread carefully—they've made me hurt like hell. É pau, é pedra, é o fim do caminho—a stick, a stone, the end of the road. No phrase could better describe what I've experienced. Forget the Tom Jobim song, these were literal sticks and stones, in my alleyways, entryways, and exits, until there were screams. Mine and theirs. Tedium had no place in that cell; it was an adult playground for grown men. Lizards that look like dragons? I still see them, to this day, and then they tell me to forget about everything and act normal again.

As though having lizards inserted into your body multiple times is something you could erase from your memory or ignore during the interview for that job that would help you reintegrate yourself into society. The woman across from me asked about my greatest strength and greatest weakness.

Greatest strength: my scream, which grew fainter each time a new lizard was put inside me. Greatest weakness: my scream, which grew fainter each time a new lizard was put inside me.

Screaming less gave me something akin to approval from the illustrious men who'd put me in that situation. My composure meant that their strategies were working. Screaming less also gave me something akin to disappointment from them, since my composure meant I'd become more amenable, more accustomed to the torture, which meant it should be intensified.

Now, it's summer. December means heat, which means more creatures and insects and more lizards crawling about. This, in sum, means that my chances of landing a job are basically null. It's the end of the road.

Yours,
Wanda de Souza

On the evening of Joan and Ana's eighteenth birthday

Joan

I left home with the brain of a matriarch and the body of a medusa. My tongue burned, ready to spew hot words. My strands of hair were antennas to the galaxies, my organs connected to simmering languages. I possessed gender and sky, a veil and a woman with an urgent look in her eye who I didn't know but felt close to. If I adjusted this blend of realities, I could touch her with my purposeful steps. The highway ahead bloomed with flowers in times past, and it was an excellent road to walk on.

Ana

It was a day of so many sounds and so few words. The phone rang, the doorbell chimed, horns honked outside the window. The cries of a grieving world affected me, shaping the way I saw of myself: I wore a skirt with so many flounces that I'd never be able to pick them up and figure out what was left of me—crude flesh, never enough, and purple-colored petals concealing fire. I was incandescent and petrified, my hair curled, twisted on iron heated with embers. The hairdresser who works Friday afternoons became my fairy godmother, the curling iron her magic wand.

Joan

Eighteen years. Like skirts layered one on top of the next, you could lift them if you want to. My dress was made of long sheaths of fabric, arranged in layers, surrounding translucence. Ascendant, I cleared the pathways within me starting with my throat, which was a volcano that harbored the fire of the century. Something that hot helps you intuit everything around you. It can influence the dreams of entire villages, give witches goosebumps, and at that moment, it pulled me to meet her.

Ana

My father kissed me on my forehead in a blessing that would last me a lifetime. Everyone took their bets on the lottery that's a woman's body. Some were optimistic, others regretful about unavoidable misfortunes; meanwhile, the one suffering the rush of opinions had little or nothing to say on the subject. Men manage property, currencies, and natural resources; they think themselves similarly capable of managing our territories.

Joan

Imagine it were possible to name Earth's inner layers—that's how I felt that day, a planet with eighteen names, eighteen stages, eighteen forms of expression. I was ready to take on the many faces I needed to become a woman. As for grandma, I don't know how many layers she contains, but I wouldn't be surprised to hear they were infinite. There were no limits to such a monumental force. That night, when you and I met, I represented the phases of Earth's evolution, condensed into a young body. I never saw my grandmother again, but I could feel her accumulate inside of me, her rotational path buried within my atoms.

Ana

The song made the room shake. *Amigos para siempre* meant it was time for crying and singing and clasping hands in a circle, but I stayed quiet. In those circumstances, my voice would be a roar, a profane sound that I carried in my belly button, in my guts, in the stuff of me that made up an eighteen-year-old at the edge of the abyss of becoming a woman. If I so much as opened my mouth, I'd release thunder at such a volume that it would empty the room. Maybe all of the guests and the band would collapse, careening towards the bottom of the pit of death, and only I'd remain, my dress like armor, my curls and legs like doors with no lock. While presiding over the unconscious staging of this promising woman-spectacle, I only allowed myself to weave between trays of snacks and sweets, searching for a new kind of life, one that would serve me.

A girl in a green dress walked towards me. When she reached me, she asked if I wanted to dance.

FONO
GRAF

1. **Eileen Myles**—*Aloha/irish trees* (LP)

2. **Rae Armantrout**—*Conflation* (LP)

3. **Alice Notley**—*Live in Seattle* (LP)

4. **Harmony Holiday**—*The Black Saint and the Sinnerman* (LP)

5. **Susan Howe & Nathaniel Mackey**—*STRAY: A Graphic Tone* (LP)

6. **Annelyse Gelman & Jason Grier**—*About Repulsion* (EP)

7. **Joshua Beckman**—*Some Mechanical Poems To Be Read Aloud* (print)

8. **Dao Strom**—*Instrument/ Traveler's Ode* (print; cassette tape)

9. **Douglas Kearney & Val Jeanty**—*Fodder* (LP)

10. **Mark Leidner**—*Returning the Sword to the Stone* (print)

11. **Charles Valle**—*Proof of Stake: An Elegy* (print)

12. **Emily Kendal Frey**—*LOVABILITY* (print)

13. **Brian Laidlaw and the Family Trade**—*THIS ASTER: adaptations of Emile Nelligan* (LP)

14. **Nathaniel Mackey and The Creaking Breeze Ensemble**—*Fugitive Equation* (compact disc)

15. *FE Magazine* (print)

16. **Brandi Katherine Herrera**—*MOTHER IS A BODY* (print)

17. **Jan Verberkmoes**—*Firewatch* (print)

18. **Krystal Languell**—*Systems Thinking with Flowers* (print)

19. **Matvei Yankelevich**—*Dead Winter* (print)

20. **Cody-Rose Clevidence**—*Dearth & God's Green Mirth* (print)

21. **Hilary Plum**—*Hole Studies* (print)

22. **John Ashbery**—*Live at Sanders Theatre, 1976* (LP)

23. **Alice Notley**—*The Speak Angel Series* (print)

24. **Alice Notley**—*Early Works* (print)

25. **Joshua Marie Wilkinson**—*Trouble Finds You* (print)

26. **Timmy Straw**—*The Thomas Salto* (print)

27. **Audre Lorde**—*At Fassett Studio, 1970* (LP)

28. **Gabriel Palacios**—*A Ten Peso Burial For Which Truth I Sign* (print)

29. **Isabel Zapata, trans. Robin Myers**—*A Whale Is a Country* (print)

30. **Callum Angus**—*Cataract* (print)

31. **Eds. Dao Strom & Jyothi Natarajan**—*A Mouth Holds Many Things: A De-Canon Hybrid-Literary Collection* (print)

32. **Cody-Rose Clevidence**—*The Grimace of Eden, Now* (print)

33. **Jaydra Johnson**—*Low: Notes on Art and Trash* (print)

34. **Jaime Gil de Biedma, trans. James Nolan**—*If Only For a Moment (I'll Never Be Young Again)* (print)

35. **Esther Kondo Heller**—*AR:RANGE:MENTS* (print)

36. **Ahmad Almallah**—*Wrong Winds* (print)

37. **Kimberly Alidio**—*Traceable Relation* (print)

38. **Sara Gilmore**—*The Green Lives* (print)

39. **Darcie Dennigan**—*Little Neck* (print)

40. **Nora Claire Miller**—*Groceries* (print)

41. **Rachel Rahmé**—*Mercurial, or Is That Liberty?* (print)

42. **Eileen Myles**—*Bird Watching and Their First Three Books of Poetry* (print)

43. **Kristen Gleason**—*The Wallet and Other Thefts* (print)

44. **Xuela Zhang**—*To Compare* (print)

45. **Cris Judar, trans. Lara Norgaard**—*They Marched Under the Sun* (print)

46. **Mark Leidner**—*Elegy for Pangaea* (print)

Fonograf Editions is a registered 501(c)(3) nonprofit organization. Find more information about the press at: fonografeditions.com.